This book belongs to:

....

This book is dedicated to you, little reader!
You are the gift the world needed and you deserve good gifts; good books. May your days be filled with wonder, joy, amazement, creativity, and peace. Read on, little one, read on!
And to Corinne & Cali, you are brave little explorers.
You inspire me.

By J. Christin Fields

Illustrated by
Natalie Vasilica

"Chocolate and Snicker, Peanut Butter and Raisin! Mom's cookies are done and YES, they're amazing!"

"Now you little fingers,
keep to yourselves tonight.
These cookies we'll eat
when the time is right."

"Off to bed and brush your teeth.
Tomorrow little people,
these cookies we'll eat."

The next sunny morning,
before breakfast began,
Mom checked on her cookies and
wondered where they all ran.

"Honey, did you eat these cookies?
They were all laying here!"
"No, I did not. I'm not the culprit dear."

"Which of you little ones has crumbs on your thumbs? Little twins, eldest two? Let the truth through your gums!"

"Not me!"

"Not me!"

"I heard a wail in the middle of the night.
A ghost ate them all, all in one bite!"

"A ghost little one? Is that so?
I am surprised to see,
your nose doesn't grow!"

"Let's be honest and tell the truth.
No. There's no cookie eating spook."
"But I heard it, I did!
Then, under the covers I hid."

Again, the sun rose.
And Mom yelled, "OH NO!"

To the kitchen everyone ran to see.
An empty tray, an empty cookie sheet.

The youngest twin began to babble,
"I heard the wail and then a rattle."

"All to your rooms,
come up with proof!"
"This time I'll catch this
munching spoof!"

The kids gave Mom their plan, to clear their name.
"We will record this ghost and put it to shame."

That night they all hid, one beside another.
Sisters and brothers,
hiding behind their taping Mother.
And the noise, like a shout, it was so loud!
The ghost approached and let out its ghouly sound.

It moaned and it growled as it
came to the kitchen,
And found the new cookies that
Mom said she'd hidden.

Mom moved in closely
to get a clear picture.
And as she moved closer,
she startled the apparitioner.

The kids hit the lights and
there stood on the floor.
Their Dad sleep walking.
The noise was his snore!

And Mom with her camera saw the story unfold.
It was Dad all along. So her apology she sold.

That morning bursts of laughter filled the room.
Dad spoke up, "And I thought I was the loon!"

Mom gave Dad her phone
and his jaw dropped.

"Guess the kids didn't do it.
It was their sleep walking Pop!"

Giggles filled the air and Dad said his peace.
"What can I say? 'Ghost-Dads' gotta eat!"

Made in the USA
Monee, IL
07 October 2020